W9-CAR-199

Where Are You From?

For Julián, Magalí, Joaquín, Areli, & Valentino
—Y.S.M.

For kids from everywhere
—J.K.

No part of this publication may be reproduced, stored in a retrieval system, or transmitted in any form or by any means, electronic, mechanical, photocopying, recording, or otherwise, without written permission of the publisher. For information regarding permission, write to HarperCollins Children's Books, a division of HarperCollins Publishers, 195 Broadway, New York, NY 10007.

ISBN 978-1-338-71301-5

Text copyright © 2019 by Yamile Saied Méndez. Illustrations copyright © 2019 by Jimyung Kim. All rights reserved. Published by Scholastic Inc., 557 Broadway, New York, NY 10012, by arrangement with HarperCollins Children's Books, a division of HarperCollins Publishers. SCHOLASTIC and associated logos are trademarks and/or registered trademarks of Scholastic Inc.

The publisher does not have any control over and does not assume any responsibility for author or third-party websites or their content.

12 11 10 9 8   23 24 25

Printed in the U.S.A.   40

First Scholastic printing, September 2020

The artist used watercolors and digital techniques to create the digital illustrations for this book.
Typography by Erica De Chavez

Where Are You From?

by **Yamile Saied Méndez** · illustrated by **Jaime Kim**

SCHOLASTIC INC.

Where are you from?
they ask.

Is your mom from here?

Is your dad from there?
they ask.

I'm from here, from today,
same as everyone else, I say.

No, where are you
really from? they insist.

I ask Abuelo because he knows everything,

and like me, he looks like he doesn't belong.

Abuelo thinks.
His eyes squint, like he's looking
inside his heart for an answer.

You come from the Pampas,

the open, free land, he says.

You're from the gaucho,
brave and strong.

From the brown river that cleanses and feeds the land
that gives us the grain for our bread, the milk from the cows.

You're from mountains so high
they tickle Señor Cielo's belly,

where the condor roosts his family
and the jaguar prowls the night.

But you're also from the warm, blue oceans
the copper warriors tried to tame

and the elegant palm trees
stretch their fingers to caress.

You're from hurricanes and dark storms,

and a tiny singing frog that calls the island people
home when the sun goes to sleep.

From this land where our ancestors built a home for all,

even when they were in chains because of the color of their skin.

You're from the grandmothers who search for their grandchildren, waiting, always waiting in a plaza, their white handkerchiefs wrapping the sorrow of their thoughts.

You come from the sunshine that lights our path in this world and the rain that washes away our mistakes.

25 MAYO 1810

But, Abuelo, I ask,
where am I really from?

Abuelo laughs.
You want a place?

He points to his heart. You're from here,

from my love and the love of all those before us,

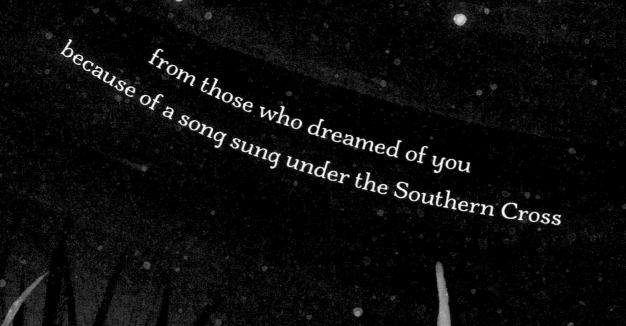

from those who dreamed of you
because of a song sung under the Southern Cross

or the words in a book written under the light of the North Star.

You?

You are from all of us.

I am.

YAMILE

(pronounced sha-MEE-lay)

SAIED MÉNDEZ

was born and raised in Rosario, Argentina, in a family with roots from all over the world. She now lives in a small mountain town in the United States with her Puerto Rican husband, five multicultural kids, two bilingual dogs, and a herd of deer that love to eat her flowers. She's a graduate of the Vermont College of Fine Arts.

JAIME KIM

was born and raised in South Korea before moving to the United States when she was eighteen. Although she was a timid child who was afraid of just about everything, she discovered a sense of serenity in drawing. As a grown-up, Jaime has finally stopped being afraid of everything but has kept on drawing and painting. She works with gouache and acrylics to create nostalgic and dreamlike illustrations, inspired by childhood memories of her family, as well as movies, art, and the outside world. Her debut picture book, *Take Heart, My Child* by Ainsley Earhardt, was a #1 *New York Times* bestseller. Jaime is also the illustrator of Kate DiCamillo's *La La La*.